This book is a work of fiction. Any references to historical events, real people, or real places are used fictitiously. Other names, characters, places, and events are products of the author's imagination, and any resemblance to actual events or places or persons, living or dead, is entirely coincidental.

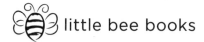 little bee books

An imprint of Bonnier Publishing USA
251 Park Avenue South, New York, NY 10010
Copyright © 2017 by Bonnier Publishing USA
All rights reserved, including the right of
reproduction in whole or in part in any form.
LITTLE BEE BOOKS is a registered trademark of Bonnier Publishing USA,
and associated colophon is a trademark of Bonnier Publishing USA.
Manufactured in the United States of America LB 1216
ISBN: 978-1-4998-0392-1 (hc)
ISBN: 978-1-4998-0391-4 (pbk)
First Edition 10 9 8 7 6 5 4 3 2 1

Library of Congress Cataloging-in-Publication Data
Names: Pearl, Alexa, 1967– author. | Sordo, Paco, illustrator.
Title: Journey beyond the trees / by Alexa Pearl; illustrated by Paco Sordo.
Description: New York, New York: Little Bee Books, [2017] | Series: Tales of Sasha; #2
Identifiers: LCCN 2016014988 | ISBN 978-1-4998-0391-4 (pbk) | ISBN 978-1-4998-0392-1 (hc)
Subjects: | CYAC: Horses—Fiction. | Animals, Mythical—Fiction. | Identity—Fiction. | Magic—Fiction. | BISAC: JUVENILE FICTION / Readers / Chapter Books. | JUVENILE FICTION / Animals / Horses. | JUVENILE FICTION / Animals / Mythical. Classification: LCC PZ7.1.P425 Jo 2017 | DDC [Fic]—dc23
LC record available at https://lccn.loc.gov/2016014988

littlebeebooks.com
bonnierpublishingusa.com

Tales of
SASHA

Journey Beyond the Trees

by Alexa Pearl
illustrated by Paco Sordo

little bee books

Contents

1. Show Me Your Wings 1

2. Watch Me Fly! 13

3. Sapphire 27

4. The Magical Map 39

5. Through the Trees 49

6. Help Is on the Way 61

7. Eyes on Me 73

8. Behind the Gold Door 85

Show Me Your Wings

"Guess what!" cried Sasha.

Her hooves kicked up clumps of grass as she trotted across the field. She stopped in front of her two sisters, Zara and Poppy. They stood in the shade of the big cottonwood tree.

"Guess what!" she cried again. Sasha was terrible at keeping secrets.

Zara didn't answer. She was busy. "Away . . . play . . . say . . . ," she said quietly. She was writing a poem. She needed the perfect rhyming word.

Poppy didn't answer. She was busy too. Poppy swatted flies with her tail. The flies flew around the flowers in her long mane.

Sasha let out a whinny. She hated when her sisters didn't listen to her.

Zara was the oldest sister. She had a jet-black coat and a chestnut-brown mane and tail. Poppy was the middle sister. She had a chestnut-brown coat and a jet-black mane and tail. Sasha was the youngest sister. She was all gray, except for a white patch on her back. She always felt like the plain sister, but not today.

Today, Sasha felt superspecial, and she had to tell her sisters why. Her secret was too exciting to keep to herself. "I have wings!" cried Sasha.

That did it. Zara spoke up. "You don't have wings. You're a horse, not a bird."

"I'm a horse with wings," said Sasha. Poppy laughed. "Is this a game?"

"No! This is real," said Sasha. "Yesterday, Wyatt and I hiked to the top of Mystic Mountain."

"Why did you and Wyatt go up there?" asked Zara.

"We went to eat wildflowers," said Sasha, "but I fell off the mountain!" Sasha shivered, remembering how scared she'd felt. "Wings popped out from the white patch on my back. Real wings!" cried Sasha. "I flew around and around."

Zara snorted. "You're making that up. Where are they now?"

"I'm telling the truth," said Sasha. "My wings went away after I flew back to the mountain."

"I want to see them," said Poppy. "Show us your wings."

Sasha had always known she was different from the horses in their valley. She dreamed of visiting far-off places. She ran the fastest and jumped the highest. Now she was different in the most amazing way. She had wings!

Sasha walked into the open field. She watched the birds flutter in the sky.

Come out, wings, she thought.

She waited.

"Wings, wings, wings," she repeated.

Nothing happened.

Maybe I need to move, she thought. Sasha began to trot.

No wings came out.

She looked over at her sisters. Zara listed more rhyming words. "Stay . . . way . . ." Poppy swatted a fly with her tail. They didn't believe she had wings.

She had to show them! She ran faster.

Still no wings.

Suddenly, she had the worst thought. *What if my wings never come out again?*

Sasha picked up speed. She galloped past Caleb, her teacher at school. Sasha couldn't slow down to say hello.

She raced past a group of trees. She spotted a large branch on the ground, and her white patch began to itch. She knew this feeling. Her white patch itched when her body wanted to jump. Her legs sprang off the ground. A cool breeze flowed through her mane as she soared high over the branch.

Sasha didn't come back down.

She looked to the left and saw clouds. She looked to the right and saw birds. She looked at her back—and saw two beautiful wings!

"She's flying!" her sisters cried from down below. "Sasha can really fly!"

Sasha flapped her wings again and again. The silver feathers sparkled in the sunlight. She wasn't the plain sister anymore!

She flapped faster, and her body tilted sideways. The valley swirled below her, making her dizzy. Whoa! She took a deep breath and straightened. She flapped her wings more slowly, letting her body glide. She flew in a huge circle. She darted through a cloud. Sasha was having so much fun!

Sasha waved her tail at her sisters on the ground. They waved their tails back at her.

Sasha lowered her neck and came in for a bumpy landing. Her hooves kicked up a spray of dirt.

Zara and Poppy crowded around. "That was amazing!" cried Zara.

"Hey, Zara, maybe it's a sister thing," said Poppy. "Watch me fly!"

Poppy trotted. Then, with a burst of energy, she flung herself at the sky. She stretched her legs out to the side and—*splat*! She landed in a split on the ground.

Zara helped Poppy up. "I guess it's not a sister thing."

Poppy touched Sasha's wings with her nose. In a flash, Sasha's wings disappeared into her back.

"You're magic!" cried Poppy. "Make them come out again."

"It doesn't work that way," said Sasha.

"How does it work?" asked Zara.

"I have no idea," said Sasha. A lot about flying and having wings didn't make sense to her.

Zara nuzzled Sasha. "Maybe they'll come out if I press you here . . . or here . . ."

"You're tickling me!" Sasha said with a giggle. Then she became serious. Should she tell them her secret story? Zara and Poppy were her sisters, after all.

"I can fly because I don't come from here," Sasha told them.

"That's crazy. Our herd has always lived in Verdant Valley," said Zara. "Ask Mom and Dad."

"I did," said Sasha. "They told me about the day I came here. There was a big storm. You were both babies, and Mom and Dad huddled with you under Mystic Mountain to keep out of the rain. Then there was a flash of lightning, and I appeared on the ground. I was wrapped in a golden blanket, and this note was with me."

Sasha pushed aside a pile of rocks under the cottonwood tree and pulled out the note.

Zara read it aloud. "'Please keep Sasha safe until we can see her again.'"

Poppy was confused. "Who wrote that? Where did you come from?"

Sasha shrugged. She had so many questions and no answers.

"Let's find Mom and Dad," said Zara. "They're at the Drinking Place."

The three sisters hurried over to the stream. The stream started high up on Mystic Mountain and flowed down into their valley. The cool water tasted best at the Drinking Place, where the stream divided into two. Their herd gathered here, especially when the weather was warm.

Sasha spotted their mom and dad.
They were alone.

"Sasha can fly!" cried Zara and Poppy.
Her parents were excited and proud.

"Tell us how," said her dad. He knew how the flowers grew and how the bees made honey. He liked to understand how things worked.

"I don't know," said Sasha. "My wings didn't come with instructions."

"Well, someone must know," said Zara.

Her mom shook her head. "Our herd has never known a flying horse."

Sasha's ears pricked up. She heard hoof beats. "Who's there?" she called.

Caleb stepped off the path and came to her. "I saw you fly!"

Sasha gulped. Was she in trouble? "You're not the only one, Sasha," said Caleb. "Other horses can fly."

Sapphire

"You—you can fly?" Sasha asked Caleb.

"Not me," said Caleb. "I once met a horse who could fly."

Sasha was so happy. She wasn't the only one! "Really? When?"

"I was just a foal," said Caleb.

Sasha looked at Caleb. His copper coat was turning gray. His back sloped with old age. He had been a foal a long time ago!

Caleb told his story. "I was playing by myself near the big trees. Suddenly, a foal with wings dropped from the sky! Her wing was hurt and that made her fall. I patched her up with bark and tree sap."

Sasha's mom nodded. Caleb was known for his kindness.

"Did she have wings like mine?" asked Sasha.

"Yes. Her wings were bright blue, and her name was Sapphire," said Caleb. "She was my friend."

"What happened to Sapphire?" asked Sasha's dad.

"Her wing healed quickly. She left that night. I never saw her again." Caleb looked sad. "I told my friends and family about her. No one believed me. They thought I was making her up."

"You weren't. She was real!" cried Sasha. "Like me!"

"She was like you. You both have the same sparkly spirit. You both dream big dreams," said Caleb. "I've always liked that about you."

Sasha was surprised. Caleb often scolded her in class for daydreaming or not following the rules. She had been sure Caleb didn't like her.

"I have so many questions for Sapphire. I have to find her!" Sasha searched the sky.

"When Sapphire left, she didn't fly. She walked through the big trees," said Caleb.

Sasha hurried in the direction of the big trees.

"No! You can't go there."
Her mother blocked her path.

"Why not?" asked Sasha, but she already knew the answer. The horses in Verdant Valley had a strict rule: Never go beyond the big trees. No one could ever tell her what was back there.

"It's just the way it is," said her mother.

"Besides, you're too little to go anywhere alone," said her father.

Sasha wouldn't give up. "Someone could come with me." Other flying horses were out there somewhere. She just knew it.

"Plus, you don't know how to find her," added her mother.

"I may know," said Caleb. "Sapphire gave me a gift before she left. She asked me not to show it to anyone, but I will show Sasha now."

He began to walk slowly through the tall grass. Sasha's parents nodded for her to follow. They stayed behind with Zara and Poppy.

Sasha walked alongside Caleb. It wasn't easy to walk as slowly as he did. On the way, she told him the story of how she'd come to the valley.

Finally, he stopped at an old pine tree. The tree had a large, dark hole in its trunk. Caleb plunged his head all the way inside.

Sasha heard rustling noises. Were those leaves? Then she heard a screech. Did he wake a sleeping owl?

"Caleb! Are you okay?" cried Sasha.

He pulled his head out. Sasha's eyes grew wide.

Between his teeth, he held a brilliant blue feather. Its glittery tip crackled with silver light.

"That feather belonged to Sapphire," whispered Sasha.

The Magical Map

Caleb placed Sapphire's blue feather on the grass. A piece of gold fabric was wrapped around the feather's stem. A thin chain held the fabric in place, and a tiny bell hung on the chain.

Caleb unhooked the chain with his teeth. The bell rang. Suddenly, a corner of the fabric poked up. Twisting and turning, the fabric began to unroll off the feather—all by itself!

Sasha watched with her mouth open.
The tiny piece of fabric grew bigger
and bigger. Soon, a huge sheet of gauzy
gold floated in the sunlight.

"Look!" cried Caleb.

Pictures magically lifted off the fabric. Buds blossomed into huge flowers. Strawberries, oranges, lemons, limes, and blueberries let out bursts of color that turned into a rainbow. Butterflies and fairies spun in dizzy circles. Sasha heard the rush of cool water and the sweet melody of a flute.

"What's this?" she asked.

"It's a magical map," said Caleb.

"A map of where?" Sasha had never seen this kind of color and beauty around here.

"Someplace far away," said Caleb. "Sapphire gave it to me. She said to first go through the big trees, and then follow the map to where she lives."

"Does the map work?" asked Sasha.
"I've never found out," said Caleb.
"You didn't go look for Sapphire?" Sasha was surprised.

"I tried once." Caleb snorted angrily. "I couldn't get through the big trees, because they were pushed together to make a wall. They wouldn't let me pass."

Sasha's stomach twisted. This was terrible news. "How can I find Sapphire if I can't walk through the trees?" she asked.

"You're not from our valley. You weren't born here. Maybe the trees will let you through," said Caleb.

Sasha felt hopeful. "Will you come with me?"

"The trees wouldn't let me in," Caleb reminded her.

"Maybe they'll let us go together. Please?" begged Sasha.

Caleb didn't answer right away. Instead, he lifted the tiny bell and rang it. *Whoosh!* The flute stopped playing. The floating pictures disappeared. The golden fabric shrunk and wrapped itself back around the stem of the blue feather.

Caleb hooked the chain to keep the magical map in place. He tucked the feather behind Sasha's left ear.

"We're going to need this map later," he said.

"We?" asked Sasha. Her heart beat quickly.

"Yes." Caleb shook his head, as if he couldn't believe he was doing this. "I'll meet you tomorrow at sunrise."

"We're going to find Sapphire!" Sasha did a little dance. "Thank you!"

"Don't thank me yet," warned Caleb. "First, we'll need to make it through the trees."

Sasha nuzzled her mom early the next morning as the first rays of sun broke through the darkness. Her sisters slept nearby. Her dad was already out looking for grazing pastures for the herd.

"Come home soon," whispered her mother. She slicked back Sasha's forelock with her tongue. "I'll be waiting for you. We all will. We love you."

"I love you too." Sasha nuzzled closer. For a moment, she thought about staying under the cottonwood tree with her family. Then she felt Sapphire's feather tucked behind her ear. This was her big chance to find other flying horses. *I have to be brave*, she thought.

Sasha set off across the field. The grass was damp with morning dew. No horses were grazing this early.

Sasha spotted Caleb up ahead. Then she stopped. Who was standing next to Caleb? She trotted closer.

"Wyatt!" she cried. "What are *you* doing here?"

"Poppy told me what you're up to. My dad said I could go too," said Wyatt. "Best friends always have adventures together."

"That's true!" Sasha was glad Wyatt was coming with them.

"Are you ready?" Caleb asked them.

"Yeah!" cried Wyatt.

Sasha nodded. She didn't want to tell them that she felt a little scared.

Caleb walked forward. Wyatt walked behind him. Sasha walked behind Wyatt. Leaves and twigs crunched under their hooves. Sunlight peeked through the branches overhead. Birds sang in the treetops. Sasha hummed along. They walked for a long time.

Suddenly, it became quiet. The birds had stopped singing. The sky turned dark.

Sasha looked up and gasped. The branches stretched toward one another, blocking the sun. "G-g-guys, the trees are moving!" cried Sasha.

The tree trunks lined up side by side. They made a wall.

Caleb tried to walk forward, but he was pushed back. He tried again and again. "I can't do it." Sweat dripped into his eyes. "You need to try, Sasha."

Sasha shivered. She took a tiny step forward.

"Keep going!" called Wyatt.

Sasha took another step. Then another and another. The sun began to shine again. The birds began to sing again.

She was doing it! The trees were parting. They were letting her through!

"I see the way. Grab on to my tail," she called to Wyatt and Caleb. "I can lead us."

"I can't go," said Caleb.

Sasha whirled around. "What's wrong?"

"My knees hurt. I'm tired," he said. "I will only slow you down."

"No way! I need you," cried Sasha.

Caleb shook his head. "Not anymore. The trees opened for you. You have Wyatt. You have the map. I'll rest here. You will be fine."

Sasha's heart pounded. She'd never gone anywhere on her own. She didn't even understand how the map worked.

Wyatt nudged her forward. "I'd bet Sapphire is right on the other side of the trees."

Sasha felt her white patch itch. It only did that when her body wanted to go. Did that mean the flying horses really were near?

She made up her mind. "We can do this," she told Wyatt. Wyatt held on to her tail with his teeth. Together, they walked toward the trees.

The trees moved to let them pass.

"We're doing it!" Sasha called to Wyatt.

Wyatt didn't answer. He didn't dare let go of her tail.

Sasha walked faster. She wanted to get them out of the creepy woods quickly. Finally, they stepped into a field of wildflowers.

"It's beautiful!" cried Sasha. The flowers pulsed with neon colors that were almost too bright for her eyes.

"It's delicious!" cried Wyatt. He began to munch. Wyatt loved to eat flowers. Sasha danced in and out of the electric flowers. She bent down to smell them.

"Wyatt!" she cried. "The red flowers smell like cherry. The yellow flowers smell like lemon. The pink flowers smell like cotton candy."

"They taste like how they smell," called Wyatt. His mouth was full of flowers.

"We need to find Sapphire," Sasha said to remind Wyatt. She pulled the blue feather from behind her ear. She opened the chain, and the tiny bell rang. The golden map magically unwrapped in the air.

"What do you see?" called Wyatt.

Sasha puzzled over the picture shimmering in front of her. "It's blue and moving. I see waves. It must be water."

"It's a lake." Wyatt came over. "There's an arrow on the lake. That arrow means we need to go across the lake."

Sasha turned in a circle. "What lake?"

"Over there." Wyatt pointed to a lake at the end of the flower field. "Race you. On your mark, get set—"

"Go!" Sasha took off.

Wyatt was fast, but she was faster. They galloped to the shore of a big lake.

Wyatt dipped his hoof into the warm water. "This lake is huge. We can't swim across."

"I could try to fly across," said Sasha.

"What about me?" asked Wyatt. "Could I hold on to your tail and fly too?"

"I don't think so." Trying to fly with Wyatt sounded hard. She'd surely crash.

"I won't leave you behind," she promised. Then she sighed. "We're stuck."

"We need help," agreed Wyatt.

"Help is on the way!"

"Who said that?" asked Wyatt.

Sasha pointed. Something was moving across the lake toward them.

Wyatt squinted. "It looks like a huge raft."

"It's a raft made out of tree trunks," said Sasha.

They watched the raft move closer and closer. Three beavers stood on the raft. They paddled it up to the shore.

"Ahoy!" called a beaver wearing a navy captain's hat. "Are you here for the noon crossing?"

"Is it noon?" asked Sasha. She had never been good at telling time.

"The sun is high. It's time to sail," said the captain. "Be quick. Hop on."

Sasha turned to Wyatt. "Should we?"

"Let's do it!" Wyatt stepped onto the raft.

"Why not?" Sasha joined him.

"Onward!" called the captain. All three beavers began to paddle, and the raft glided across the lake.

Eyes on Me

"Did Sapphire send you?" Sasha asked the captain hopefully.

"No one sent me," he said. "The ferry is on a schedule. It goes every hour. Sometimes every two hours. Sometimes I take a nap. Then it doesn't go."

"That doesn't sound like a good schedule," said Sasha.

"I'm glad it wasn't nap time," Wyatt pointed out. "Sasha wanted to fly, but I can't."

The captain poked Sasha with his paddle. "You're a winged one!"

"You've seen them!" cried Sasha. That was a good sign. "Where are they?"

"I'm a water-and-wood guy. I don't know what happens in the sky." He began to paddle again.

"Row, row, row, your boat," he sang. The other beavers joined in. Their oars pushed through the water as they sang.

When the song ended, the captain steered the raft to a dock. He hurried Sasha and Wyatt off. A family of foxes got on.

"Wait!" called Sasha. The captain hadn't told her where to go.

"Ticktock!" called the captain. "No time to chat." The three beavers paddled the raft away.

"I hope the flying horses are close by," Sasha told Wyatt. "Let's check the map."

She unhooked the chain. The bell rang, and the magic map opened. Sasha reared back. Hundreds of eyes swirled before them! Blinking. Winking. Staring. Eyes were everywhere.

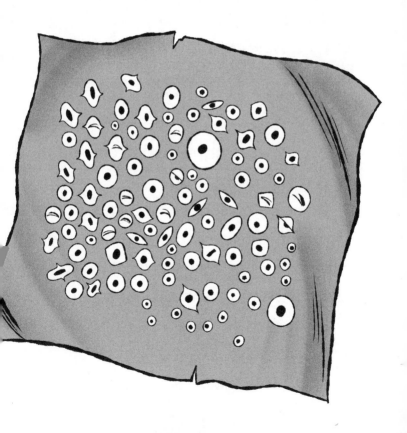

Wyatt squeezed his eyes shut. "I don't like all those eyes looking at me. Maybe we should try to go back."

Sasha was surprised. Wyatt had never acted scared before.

"I can't give up now," she said. The thought of the flying horses nearby had made her feel braver. She rang the tiny bell and the map rolled up again. The eyes went away. "We need to find eyes," she told Wyatt. "I need your eyes to look for eyes."

Wyatt opened one eye and then the other. Then he followed Sasha. She walked in front.

They passed three rabbits playing hopscotch.

They passed two flamingos on a tightrope.

They passed a turtle flying a kite.

"I knew beyond the trees would be special," said Sasha.

"This place is nothing like home," said Wyatt.

Suddenly, she stopped short. Wyatt tumbled into her.

"All eyes on me!" cried a bright blue peacock. He strutted before them. "Do you see what I see?"

"What does he see?" Sasha whispered to Wyatt.

"You need more eyes to see what I see," said the large bird.

"More eyes?" Wyatt didn't like the sound of that.

The peacock lifted his tail and opened a huge fan of emerald-green feathers. Each feather had an eye-shaped spot in the middle.

"He has eyes on his feathers!" cried Wyatt. "The map wanted us to find this peacock."

"Do you know where Sapphire is?" asked Sasha.

"Look and see." The peacock grinned. "A bird's-eye view is always best."

"Everything is a riddle here," Wyatt said with a grumble.

Sasha looked closely. Every feather looked the same—except one. One feather was bright blue, not green. It didn't have an eye-shaped spot. It looked exactly like the feather Sapphire had given Caleb.

"That feather isn't yours," she told the peacock. "That feather comes from the wing of a flying horse!"

Behind the Gold Door

Sasha plucked the blue feather from the peacock's tail. It had a square stem.

"Follow the feather to the winged horses," said the peacock. Then he strutted away.

"There isn't a map on this feather," said Wyatt. "How do we follow it?"

Suddenly, a strong breeze blew the feather from Sasha's mouth. The feather twirled in crazy circles. Then it zoomed forward.

For a moment, Sasha watched it. Then she remembered the peacock's words. "Follow the feather!" cried Sasha. She raced after it.

"Wait for me!" yelled Wyatt.

The feather flew to a beach. They galloped down the hot sand after it. Finally, the feather fluttered to the ground. Sasha and Wyatt stopped too. They stood in a clearing surrounded by rock walls. The sand glittered with rubies, emeralds, diamonds, and other jewels.

"Wow! My sisters would love it here," said Sasha.

Wyatt pointed to a shiny gold door in one of the rock walls. "What's that?"

Sasha walked over to it and knocked.

No answer.
She knocked harder.

Still no answer.

She pushed against it. "It's locked," she told Wyatt.

Wyatt looked at the sky. "The sun is going down. We should go home."

"Go home? Now?" Sasha couldn't believe it. "We've made it through the big trees, crossed a huge lake, and now we're here. Maybe Sapphire and the flying horses are on the other side of this door. I can't go home now!"

She unhooked the magic map and watched it unroll. A picture of an old-fashioned key floated before them. "We need to find a key," said Sasha. "A key will open the door."

Wyatt paced back and forth. "It'll be dark soon. Do you think the ferry is still running? Do you think Caleb is still by the trees?"

"Let's look fast," said Sasha. "Hurry!"

Sasha and Wyatt searched for a key in the piles of rubies and emeralds. They couldn't find one anywhere.

"We need to go," said Wyatt.

"Soon." Sasha wouldn't stop digging.

Wyatt groaned and kicked at a pile. A diamond sailed through the air and hit the gold door.

Sasha hurried over to the door. "Oh! You scratched it." Then she spotted a tiny hole. She knew that shape! "I found the keyhole. Where's the blue feather from the peacock?" she asked.

Wyatt lifted it from the ground and brought it over. "Why do you want this? Don't we need a key?"

"The feather is the key," she said.

She stuck the tip of the feather's square stem into the keyhole. *Click!*

The gold door swung open—and a horse flew out. Then another and another!

"We found the flying horses!" cried Wyatt.

Sasha sucked in her breath as they circled overhead. "They're just like me."

Wyatt looked to the sky. "That horse has yellow wings. That horse has purple wings. That horse has blue wings. It's Sapphire!"

Sasha felt her patch itch. Then every part of her body itched to fly.

"Sasha," said Wyatt, "your wings popped out!"

"Should I go up?" she asked.

"Yes! Go fly!" said Wyatt.

Sasha grinned at her best friend. Then she ran and leaped. Her wings flapped, and she soared up, up, up.

She was finally going to meet other flying horses!

Read on for a sneak peek
from the third book in the
Tales of Sasha series!

Tales of
SASHA

A New Friend

by Alexa Pearl

illustrated by Paco Sor

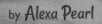

Just Like Me

"Wait for me!" cried Sasha. She tried to catch up. She flew higher. She flapped her wings faster, but she still couldn't reach them.

Thick clouds rolled in, making it hard to see. Now she didn't know which way to turn. Then Sasha's breath caught in her throat.

Three horses flew out of a large cloud! One was yellow, one was blue, and one was purple. Their colorful wings shone bright against the gray sky. They were just like her. They were horses that could fly!

Sasha had never met another flying horse before. She just *had* to talk to them—now!

The three horses darted in and out of the clouds. They flew in crazy patterns.

"Wait for me!" she called again.

The three flying horses didn't wait.

Sasha was the fastest horse in her valley. She had won every running race. But flying was different than running. Horses didn't fly in a straight line.

"Keep going!" Wyatt called to her from the beach. The sand at his hooves sparkled with magical jewels. He raised his tail in a salute.

Sasha saluted back. Wyatt was her best friend. He had traveled with her all the way from their home in Verdant

Valley to Crystal Cove, the land where the flying horses live.

"That must be Sapphire!" Wyatt pointed at the blue horse.

Sasha flapped her wings as fast as she could. She had heard stories about Sapphire, but she'd never met her. Sasha had never met *any* flying horses. Until now, she'd thought she was the only one. She had so many questions for them.

"Sapphire! I'm back!" cried Sasha.

Sapphire swooped low and out of sight.

She didn't hear me, thought Sasha.

Then Sasha spotted the yellow horse. She sped over to him.

"I just learned to fly!" she called.

The yellow horse soared high and out of sight.

He doesn't care, thought Sasha.

The purple horse zoomed by.

"Hello!" called Sasha.

The purple horse didn't answer. Instead, she tucked her head and somersaulted in the air.

Sasha gasped. That was amazing!

"Your turn," called the purple horse.

Sasha looked around. Who was she talking to?

The purple horse pointed her braided tail at Sasha.

"Me?" Sasha gulped. She didn't know if she could do gymnastics and fly at the same time.

The purple horse waited.

Was this a test? If she passed, would the purple horse answer her questions? Sasha took a deep breath. *You can do this,* she told herself. *Head first, legs in, tuck, and roll. Go!*

The world spun upside down. Wind rushed up her nostrils, and her stomach twisted. Then she was upright again and flying. She heard Wyatt cheer. She had done it!

The purple horse smiled. "Fly with me!" she called.

Together, they soared through the clouds. The warm wind blew their manes. Sasha smiled. She had made her first friend in the Land of Flying Horses.